KT-434-411

Grumpy Cat

Britta Teckentrup

Boxer Books

Once there was a cat who lived all alone.

He ate on his own.
He slept on his own.
He spent every day alone.

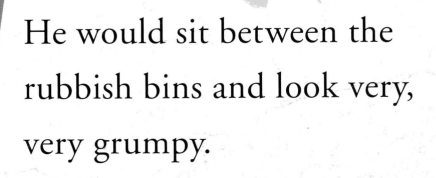

He would sit between the
rubbish bins and look very,
very grumpy.

At night, other cats in the neighbourhood
would meet and play together.
Cat wanted to join in,
but he just didn't know how.

The other cats didn't ask him because
they thought he was a grumpy cat.
But really – he was a lonely cat.

One night everything changed.
There was a terrible thunderstorm
that crashed and shook the ground.
Cat looked for shelter from the storm,
but there wasn't any.
Poor Cat got wetter, colder, soggier
and even grumpier than before.

Then suddenly, out of nowhere,
there came a miaow. Cat looked
down and there, between his paws,
was a little ginger kitten.
Kitten was as wet and as cold
and as soggy as Cat.
"Miaow," said Kitten.
Cat didn't know what to do.

The rain stopped.

Kitten miaowed again.

She thought she had found a friend.

But Cat just glared at Kitten and walked away.

Kitten followed Cat.

She rolled on her back and showed her belly.

She wiggled her tail
under Cat's nose.

She tried to catch Cat's tail.
She just wanted to be friendly.
But Cat still looked grumpy.

Cat tried his best to lose Kitten
by balancing on a high picket fence.
But Kitten was right behind him.

Cat thought he had finally lost
Kitten by climbing a tall tree.
Then Cat heard a miaow.
Slowly and grumpily, Cat turned around.
There at the foot of the tree was Kitten.

Kitten followed Cat up the tree.

She tried to reach
him by balancing
on the thinnest
of branches.

Then Kitten slipped . . .

Quick as a flash, Cat leapt over
and took Kitten gently by the scruff
of her neck and carried her down
the tree to safety.

Once they were on the ground,
Cat licked Kitten to make sure
she felt safe.

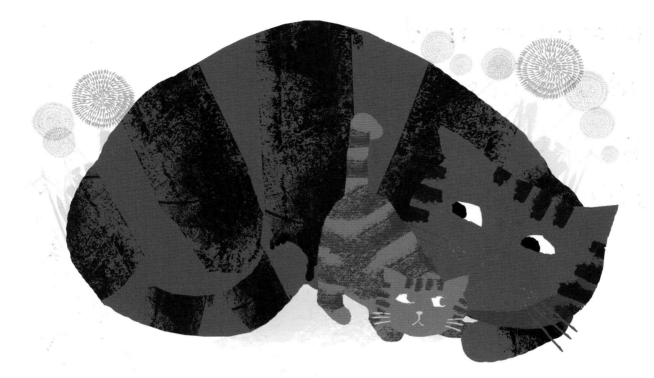

Kitten miaowed. She was happy and hungry.

Cat dashed off . . .

but soon returned
with a surprise –
a great, big, fresh fish
as big as Kitten!

Cat and Kitten ate until their bellies were full.

Cat and Kitten cuddled up for a snooze.

They had each found a friend.

And Cat was never grumpy again . . .

Well, almost never.

Other Boxer Books paperbacks

Big Smelly Bear: **Britta Teckentrup**

When Big Smelly Bear gets an itch he cannot reach, Big Fluffy Bear offers to help him out. But first, she tells him, he must take a bath. A warm story of friendship with a sweet-smelling ending.

ISBN 13: 978-1-905417-43-8

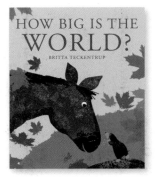

How Big is the World?: **Britta Teckentrup**

Journey to the far corners of the world with Little Mole, as he travels from the frozen north to the tropics and asks the question "how big is the world?"

ISBN 13: 978-1-905417-62-9

Tip Tip Dig Dig: **Emma Garcia**

Tip Tip Dig Dig is an inventive story for children. Each construction vehicle makes its own noise as they all work together towards a surprise ending. Perfect for reading aloud.

ISBN 13: 978-1-905417-84-1

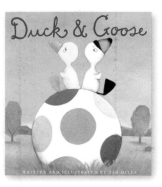

Duck & Goose: **Tad Hills**

Duck and Goose find an egg. "Who does it belong to?" they ask. Parents everywhere will recognise this tale of one-upmanship, which firmly establishes the positive aspects of learning to share.

ISBN 13: 978-1-905417-26-1

to Vincent, Oskar, and Sputnik
Britta Teckentrup

BRISTOL CITY LIBRARIES

AN1800045210	
PE	09-Oct-2008
JF	£6.99

First published in hardback Great Britain in 2008 by Boxer Books Limited.
First published in paperback Great Britain in 2008 by Boxer Books Limited.

www.boxerbooks.com

Text and illustrations copyright © 2008 Britta Teckentrup

The rights of Britta Teckentrup to be identified as the author
and illustrator of this work have been asserted by her
in accordance with the Copyright, Designs and Patents Act, 1988.

All rights reserved, including the right of reproduction in whole or in part in any form.
A CIP catalogue record for this book is available from the British Library upon request.

ISBN 13: 978-1-905417-70-4

1 3 5 7 9 10 8 6 4 2

Printed in China

All of our papers are sourced from managed forests and renewable resources.